SNOWMEN AT NIGHT

Caralyn Buehner

pictures by Mark Buehner

Phyllis Fogelman Books

New York

One wintry day I made a snowman,
very round and tall.
The next day when I saw him,
he was not the same at all!

His hat had slipped, his arms drooped down,
he really looked a fright—
it made me start to wonder:
What *do* snowmen do at night?

I think that snowmen start to slide
(when it gets *really* dark),
off the lawn and down the street—
right into the park.

They gather in a circle while they wait for all the others,
sipping cups of ice-cold cocoa, made by snowman mothers.

Then the snowman games begin: They line up in their places,
each one anxious for his turn in the snowman races.

After everyone has had a chance at racing once or twice,
they go on over to the pond to do skating tricks on ice.

Sometimes they start giggling,
and then they act like clowns—
they bump into each other,
'til they all fall down.

They gather up their snowballs, the pitcher takes his aim,
and underneath the moonlit sky they play a baseball game.

No one knows just how it started,
but soon it's quite a sight—
with snowmen throwing snowballs
in the world's best snowball fight!

Then it's time for sledding! It's a wild ride down the hill!

"WAAHOOOOOOOOOOO!"
they yell.
This is, by far, the
snowmen's biggest thrill!

Finally they're tuckered out, and getting sleepy, so
they slowly gather up their things, and one by one they go.

So if your snowman's grin is crooked,
or he's lost a little height,
you'll know he's just been doing
what snowmen do at night!

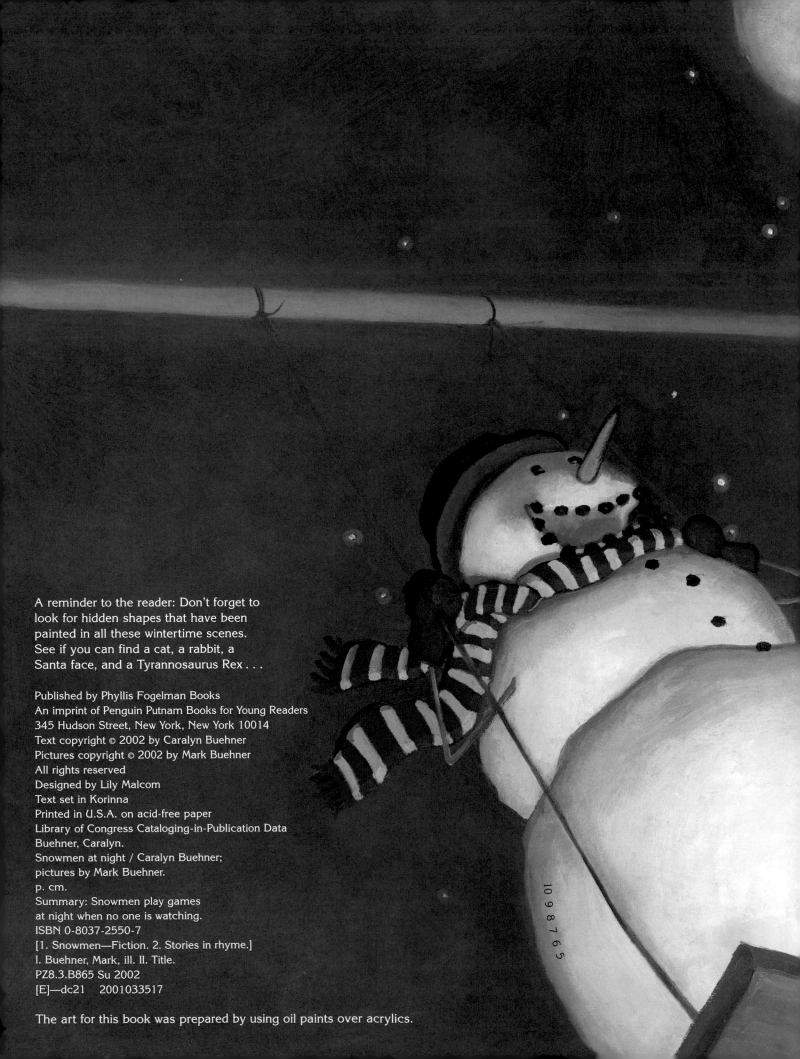

A reminder to the reader: Don't forget to
look for hidden shapes that have been
painted in all these wintertime scenes.
See if you can find a cat, a rabbit, a
Santa face, and a Tyrannosaurus Rex . . .

Published by Phyllis Fogelman Books
An imprint of Penguin Putnam Books for Young Readers
345 Hudson Street, New York, New York 10014
Text copyright © 2002 by Caralyn Buehner
Pictures copyright © 2002 by Mark Buehner
All rights reserved
Designed by Lily Malcom
Text set in Korinna
Printed in U.S.A. on acid-free paper
Library of Congress Cataloging-in-Publication Data
Buehner, Caralyn.
Snowmen at night / Caralyn Buehner;
pictures by Mark Buehner.
p. cm.
Summary: Snowmen play games
at night when no one is watching.
ISBN 0-8037-2550-7
[1. Snowmen—Fiction. 2. Stories in rhyme.]
I. Buehner, Mark, ill. II. Title.
PZ8.3.B865 Su 2002
[E]—dc21   2001033517

10 9 8 7 6 5

The art for this book was prepared by using oil paints over acrylics.

To Jay and Kris,
our surreptitious
snowman shifters